# A Case for Buffy

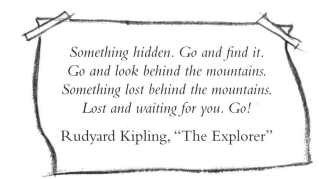

*Something hidden. Go and find it.*
*Go and look behind the mountains.*
*Something lost behind the mountains.*
*Lost and waiting for you. Go!*

Rudyard Kipling, "The Explorer"

DETECTIVE GORDON

# A Case for Buffy

BY ULF NILSSON · ILLUSTRATED BY GITTE SPEE

GECKO PRESS

# CHAPTER ONE

# A sweet little police station

In the forest was a small police station. Any animal with a problem could go there for help. It was painted red with white windowsills and had smoke coiling up from the chimney to the sky. There was a garden too, and a lawn and currant bushes.

The police station was busy on this chilly autumn morning. From inside you could hear kla-dunk, kla-dunk. It was peaceful work, though.

Outside, small figures were creeping around. They ran towards the currant bush at the corner of the house and hid themselves.

Inside the police station were two police officers: Detective Gordon and Detective Buffy. Buffy was a young mouse. At that moment she was sitting at the big desk wearing her fine police hat. She was leafing through important police papers and reading aloud from Gordon's notes (Detective Gordon, the famous criminal detective, the terror of all villains): "Hmm, Mister Badger has found a blue scarf…"

Buffy scratched behind one large ear, thinking. Then she brightened, and began to leaf through other important papers. Yes, there it was.

"Lost!" she read. "Granny Squirrel has lost her scarf and would like it back immediately (because it is getting colder). If someone finds it…"

Buffy whistled to herself. Soon she would ask the squirrel to describe the scarf. If she answered "it's blue" then the case was solved.

Buffy wrote *Crime probably solved* on the paper and took out the lovely stamp. She placed it on the paper, moved it a little to the right, a little to the left, and then she stamped so hard that the desktop sang. This was how you did police work! She stamped one more time, kla-dunk, so it could be heard even if you were standing outside—or if you were hidden in the police station's currant bushes...

"Crime and crime," she muttered to herself. She rubbed out the words and wrote *The problem is probably solved* instead. Then she stamped a third time.

Next came the case of an angry grandfather badger who had said "Snot child!" to a little mouse. That meant the police had to go in and do some educating. All the animals in the forest should be kind to one another.

If they were angry because they had woken

up on the wrong side of the bed, they should avoid other animals or at least stay quiet. The badger needed to be told (as did the little mouse, who in fact was always snotty). Kla-dunk.

The last thing Buffy had to do that day was to order new cakes for the three cake tins. A very important job. There were new kinds available: coconut tops, banana cakes with crispy sugar topping, and nougat rolls with mint chips. Buffy thought she should probably wait till Gordon was awake. It was important that everyone was kept happy. Although the banana cakes sounded very good…

How happy and pleased Buffy was! Inside she felt absolutely pink and pale blue. She took off her cap and polished it. She loved being a police officer and doing important things. She loved the police station. A sweet little police station, as she said to Gordon. She loved

the writing desk and the spinning chair and the stamp
and the sweet little prison. Yes, because the prison
was no longer a prison. It had two beds in it and the
detectives slept in them.

Suddenly she heard snoring, a really powerful
detective snore that shook the prison bars.

Two figures hidden in the currant bush now crept up
to the window and looked in. They could see a big,
puffed-up toad under the covers: Detective Gordon
lying in bed.

Gordon was dozing, as he called it. He could hear everything that was happening in the police station, every paper that rustled, every small hum or giggle, and every stamp that was stamped. He enjoyed listening to this encouraging work. But then he dozed off and dreamed a little, waking at the smallest squeak from Buffy's spinning chair. When he woke, he lay and thought. About himself, for example.

And how he, for example, was quite old. Nineteen years old. He was more tired than before and he enjoyed his bed very much. A nice pair of flannel pajamas, lovely cold sheets, a warm bedcover and a really soft pillow. Could anything be better? Gordon gave a small sigh.

He usually got up in the evening to drink tea with Buffy. And have an evening cake, of course. Then he'd sit at the desk during the night, maybe dozing off now and then, but if anyone came in wanting help he would wake up immediately.

He looked after the police station all night. Now and again he would nibble on a secret night cake. And in the morning he served morning cakes to Buffy and himself before creeping back to bed.

If something terrible happened then of course both detectives put on their police hats and went out into the forest to solve the case. But that wasn't often. Mostly police work involved a naughty child throwing litter on the meadow or a lost mole or hedgehog happening to fall asleep in the middle of the path. Nice small crimes, or at least not-nasty, as Gordon would say.

Nothing ever happened that was really bad. And the detectives were very pleased about that. Kind animals in the police district, good cakes, cold sheets. Things could hardly be better.

Gordon dozed off. He had a little mini-dream about when he was a young toad. There he was in his shorts, with a big sun hat, building a tall sandcastle. His mother stood beside him clapping her hands.

"How clever, little Gordon. I'm so proud of you!"

What a wonderful dream. Gordon woke to the sound
of Buffy's cheerful whistling. And the sound of some
creature walking outside the station, rustling leaves.

"Buffy," Gordon called. "You can't imagine the
dream I just had about my mother. She was so kind
and happy…"

Buffy's whistling stopped. She rustled a piece of paper.

"Buffy," called Gordon. "Where does your mother
live, exactly? Where is she?"

Now the paper rustling stopped too. It became absolutely quiet.

"You understand, Buffy, that mothers are very important. When you think about your mother you get all warm inside, even when you're very old..."

"Squeak," said Buffy.

And was that the small sound of sniffing?

Gordon didn't have time to think more about it, because suddenly the door burst open and two figures rushed into the police station.

# A small police school

"Here we are at last!" cried the two small figures, giggling.

It was a baby toad with a blue cap and a little baby mouse who hopped ceaselessly up and down. Gordon recognized them at once from the forest kindergarten.

"We're going to be police, we too!" squeaked the baby mouse.

"We crept here very quietly," said the baby toad.

Hmm, thought Gordon, I could hear you all the time. But he said nothing.

He slowly got out of bed and asked the two young ones to turn around while he got dressed and put on his police hat.

"Good morning, small police!" he said happily when he was ready, and he gave them a salute.

The baby toad answered with a salute, but he used the wrong hand. The little mouse went on hopping up and down in excitement.

"Good morning, big police!" squeaked the baby mouse.

Gordon had an idea. He remembered how poorly he'd done recently at interrogating children. He hadn't really understood them, that time the two little ones had disappeared. Now he had a chance to talk to some children and get to know them better. What if he could start a school, a small police school…

"Very good, small police!" said Gordon, stretching. "The first lessons of the small police school will begin in ten minutes. And we'll carry on till tomorrow. But first of all, small police must run home and ask their mothers if they are allowed to sleep overnight…"

The two of them disappeared in a flash.

"…and then they must come back here," Gordon continued to himself. "It will be good, Buffy, if I train some new police for the future. Small police, I mean."

Buffy said nothing. She sat quite still, looking down at the papers on the desk. She felt very dark inside.

Gordon filled his mouth with special cakes: apple muffins with caramel toffee. And he started to walk back and forth across the floor.

"Gruff gruff creeping, gruff gruff guard watching," he muttered and a few toffee crumbs flew from his mouth. "Hmm, salutes! That's it!"

He had been planning lessons. And exactly then his two police students returned, each carrying a backpack.

Their parents had given them permission.

"Mama has put pajamas and a toothbrush in my pack," said the young toad, whose name was Sune.

"I have to wash before I go to bed, my mother says," said the small baby mouse called Gertrude. "My mother's so nice! She gave me cheese sandwiches too."

Buffy seemed to sniff again and her head fell a little towards her chest.

Hmm, thought Gordon.

"My name is Detective Gordon." He showed which hand to use for salute.

"My name is Sune," said the baby toad, doing a very good salute.

"Police Student Sune," Gordon corrected.

"Police Student Gertrude," said the small mouse, saluting even as she jumped up and down.

"Do not hop when you are doing a salute!" said Gordon, and Gertrude stopped hopping.

After that they made a tour of the forest. They followed paths and saluted everyone they met. All the mice and frogs were very surprised to find the police force marching around their paths.

On their way back they chorused: "Good morning, ma'am, how can we help you?" to every surprised crow or mouse they met.

Lesson number one was finished; both students had managed it excellently.

The next lecture was about creeping.

"You absolutely must not giggle and you should not walk on rustly leaves," said Gordon.

18

The little ones crept three, four times around the house. Then they were given the task of spying on an old rabbit limping along the path. Where was he going?

A quarter of an hour later the police students returned to the police station.

"He went home," Gertrude and Sune reported. "He walked really slowly."

Then there was a lesson in how to watch a hole.

"I have certainly watched a few holes in my time," said Gordon, shivering at the thought. "You have to sit completely still, and stare at the hole with everlasting patience."

Gertrude and Sune watched a woodpecker's hole in a tree. After an hour's intent staring they had fulfilled their task. They were patient police students, you'd have to agree.

The last lesson of the day was about daring to investigate deep crannies. The students were each given a searchlight, and told to find a cranny and creep down into it. Off they went.

Gordon felt rather tired and lay down on his bed to rest his legs a little. Sadly, he fell asleep and dreamed about a cake his mother had baked. Not sadly that he dreamed about the cake, but sadly that he fell asleep while the young ones were out looking in crannies.

He didn't wake until the dirty youngsters came back to report that they had investigated twenty crannies, which were all completely empty, although very earthy.

*Yawn.* "Bravo," said Gordon. "Then we must make you small hats. With gold stars."

Buffy was still sitting at the desk, her head hanging and her eyes blank. She didn't seem to notice the others. The young ones spun her around in her chair, while she sat completely stiff and still.

Gordon took out a piece of thick blue paper, scissors and glue. The young ones set about making police hats for themselves. On the front they stuck a star cut out of gold paper.

"Write *WE ARE ALL POLICE!* on the gold stars," said Gordon.

The little ones each grabbed a pen and scribbled on the stars.

Of course, thought Gordon, they can't write yet.

Then the young police continued to cut out blue hats and gold stars. It was so much fun that they didn't stop until they had made twenty-five. There were a whole lot of extra police hats. Gertrude put them in her backpack.

"How clever you are!" said Gordon.

Then he came to thinking about Buffy, who had rolled her chair back into the corner. How was she? She didn't usually sit still so long, thinking.

"How are things, Buffy?"

"My mother's gone!" Buffy said quietly.

Suddenly her eyes filled and tears fell straight down her cheeks.

## Where is Mama?

The winter before, a small girl mouse, zero years old, had come to the forest. She and Detective Gordon had met while he was guarding a squirrel hole.

Afterwards she had moved into the police station, and been given the job of police assistant and a name—Buffy. (Gordon called her that because *bufo* means *toad* in Latin.) She was very talented and clever and learned everything a police officer needs to know. Later she was made Acting Chief Detective.

But what had she done before she turned up in the snowy forest? Where had she come from?

"My mother!" Buffy cried. "I lost my mother."

Then Sune and Gertrude also began to cry. Losing a mother was the worst thing they could imagine.

"Oh, poor Buffy," said Gordon sorrowfully. "Do tell us…"

"I can't tell you," she sniffed. "I've forgotten everything. Maybe I got a shock."

Hmm, was it silly of him not to have asked Buffy about this before? he wondered. Police had four questions to ask when they found someone unknown:

What's your name?

Where do you live?

What is your work?

How old are you?

Perhaps Gordon needed to add a fifth question: Where is your mother?

Except you never really knew with mice, Gordon thought. Maybe mice could leave their families and think no more about them. You couldn't assume that everyone was like a completely ordinary toad. We animals are all so different, he thought.

Sune and Gertrude were crying harder and harder at the thought of losing their mothers. Gordon had to do something.

"Now we will solve this problem! We are two detectives and two small police. How hard can it be?"

Everyone stopped crying at once.

"First, Buffy must sit down with a pen and paper in a comfortable chair with a cup of tea and a candle. Then, Buffy, you can write about how things were in your childhood."

"But I can't remember!"

All three started crying again.

"Shh!" said Gordon. "Why don't you start by writing small poems about your mother, so the memories come back. That's what a real police officer does."

Buffy sat in the armchair, Gordon lit a candle, and she began to write.

*A little mother.*
*A fir tree, a hole, a root.*
*A soft and grassy nest.*
*All our songs!*
*Many brothers, many sisters...*

"Now we'll let her sit for a minute," Gordon
whispered to the small police. "During this time we
will think about some cases. Completely normal cases.
Because serious things almost never happen here.
Normal police work is the norm!"

They talked about the case of the naughty child who had thrown litter onto the lovely meadow. What should be done about that?

"Catch the child," said Sune, "and put it in prison."

"No." Gordon shook his head so that all his chins wobbled.

"You go to the big police and tell them to catch the naughty child," suggested Gertrude.

Gordon continued to shake his head.

"You pick up the litter!" he said at last.

"But the police should punish the naughty child!" said both small police, upset. "At least scold him!"

"Yes, how can you tell someone off nicely so he does things properly the next time? A police officer must think!"

The small police thought.

"You run after him and catch him," said Gertrude.

Gordon began to shake his head carefully.

"And then you give him the rubbish," she continued, "and say, 'Excuse me, but you might have dropped this.'"

"Bravo," said Gordon. "You tell him—or her—off in a nice way so they learn."

In the meantime Buffy sat biting the end of her pencil.

*Eight little brothers and sisters*
*Plus eight big brothers and sisters.*
*Lovely.*
*Mama's warm milk.*
*Snuggly blankets...*

The next police case was about a hedgehog who had gone to sleep in the middle of the path. What should you do if you found that hedgehog?

"Go to the police!"

Gordon shook his head.

"Wake her," said Sune. "And help her find a better place to sleep."

"Bravo," said Gordon. "You don't need to go to the police for every little thing. You can simply be helpful. Everyone in the woods has to help each other. We are all citizens of our forest. We are like members of a club..."

"We are all police!" said Sune.

"Except no one has such good hats as ours," said Gertrude.

*Sleep long and warm.*
*Howling wind. A crash!*

*Snowflakes flying,*
*Roof falling…*

Buffy started to tremble. Her memories were slowly coming back. Something terrible had happened after all. A catastrophe.

"And now for the last police case," said Gordon. "Old Grandpa Badger says 'Snot child!' to a little mouse. What does the little mouse do? Think now like real police."

"It wasn't a nice thing to say," said Gertrude with feeling. "Something needs to be done."

"Like what?"

"Say, 'Stupid nasty old man!' and tell him off," said Gertrude.

"Or say that you're very sad," said Sune. "And start to cry."

*Sharp claws—Fox!*
*Running here and there.*
*Waterfall, fir trees…*
*Running all day*
*Over snow, over mountains.*
*Everyone's gone!*

*Don't stop running…*
*But where's my little mother?*

"Now I remember everything," cried Buffy. "Everything came to me in the poems."

Gordon got up and looked over her shoulder at them.

"Fox?" he said.

"Fox!" wailed both small, terrified police. "Was your mother eaten up?"

It was quiet for a moment. It had grown dark outside the police station. And it had started to rain. Drops clattered on the roof.

"Hmm, I don't think so," said Buffy.

"Hope she survived," said Gertrude. "Hope, hope."

Gordon read more of Buffy's poem. He had a lump in his throat, but he coughed.

"Waterfall and fir tree? And far away from here? Hmm, where could that be?"

He unfolded the big police map. He looked carefully and found at last an island with fir trees and a waterfall. Cave Island, it was called.

"That island, Cave Island," he said quietly, pointing. "Isn't that where the fox moved to when I drove him away?"

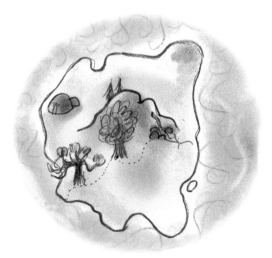

# CHAPTER FOUR

# Through the dark, over the mountain

"But it wasn't an island!" Buffy protested. "I just ran and ran over a really big field."

"That's strange," said Gordon. "Cave Island is the only place on the map with a waterfall and fir trees. And you can see clearly that there is water between here and there. Can you have forgotten the sea, do you think?"

"No, I remember everything now."

Gertrude began hopping up and down. There was something she had to say.

"Maybe the sea had frozen and you thought it was a field?"

"Bravo," said Gordon. "What luck that we have our small police!"

He nodded. "That's probably what happened. This all took place out there on the island. The same island that the fox moved to. Not good, not good at all…"

"What shall I do?" Buffy asked in confusion.

"Tomorrow we'll come up with something," answered Gordon.

Gertrude yawned. This was all so exciting, but she was tired too.

"Some of us must now go to bed," Gordon said, and he patted Gertrude on the head.

He went up to the attic to fetch the two small beds. He made them up for Sune and Gertrude.

As far as the washing went, Gordon had a plan.

The small police were each given a glass of milk and an evening cake: sugar cones dipped in icing sugar. After all that sugar they were forced to wash themselves, including the tail if they were a mouse. It was simple.

Afterwards they brushed their teeth, put on their pajamas and snuggled into their beds.

"I think I will also go to bed," said Gordon.

"Tomorrow we must talk about Cave Island and what we can do."

They all lay in the prison with their beds in a row.

"Good night," said Gordon.

"Sleep well," said Buffy.

"Good night and sleep well," said Sune.

Gertrude said nothing at all because she was already asleep.

Then Gordon turned out the light and sighed deeply. Yes, he was tired in fact.

He lay there, thinking through the case. A whole small mouse family, almost a year ago, had had its nest destroyed by a hungry fox. The mouse mother and all her children had run in different directions. Had any of them been caught and eaten by the fox? Buffy, at least, had run and run as far as she could. She had run the whole day.

What had happened then? Yes, he knew. Buffy had climbed a tree and taken nuts because she'd been so terribly hungry. Then Detective Gordon had spotted her and called, "Stop, in the name of the law!"

What a terrible way to say hello to a mouse child who had fled through storm and snow from a ghastly catastrophe. How rude of him!

But what had happened to Buffy's mother? And to her fifteen brothers and sisters? It was a long time ago now. Perhaps one should simply hope that everything had turned out well…

Gordon heard that the small police were sleeping deeply as they snored quietly. He also heard Buffy turn over in bed. Of course she couldn't sleep.

"Shall we have an extra cake, Buffy?" Gordon whispered. "A strawberry-crusted cake. Then we might find it easier to sleep."

Buffy sat straight up.

"I have to go," she said. "I have to rescue my mother."

"But," Gordon said, "it's so long since it happened!"

"All the more reason to hurry," said Buffy.

"Buffy. You can't go out looking alone."

"Yes, I can," she said. "I am in fact Chief Detective."

"Then I'll come too," said Gordon. "But it's dark!"

"There are searchlights."

"It's raining," said Gordon.

"We have raincoats."

"But who will look after the small police?"

Gordon turned on the light. He found that Sune and Gertrude were sitting up in their beds, listening to every word.

"We'll come too," said Gertrude. "I'm not tired any more!"

"Me neither," said Sune. "I've slept enough."

All the police and small police hurried out of bed and dressed. Out came proper raincoats. Out came an umbrella. Out came searchlights and the police hats.

Gertrude stood looking at the pistol, which was kept in a glass case.

"Shall we take the pistol? Bang, bang."

"Never the pistol," Buffy and Gordon said at the same time. "It will never be used."

"No?" Gertrude was disappointed.

Gordon took down the cake tins from the shelf. First he tried to put the tins into the big backpack, but they didn't fit. Then he tipped all the cakes straight into the pack, taking an almond dream cake while he was at it.

"Please hurry," said Buffy. "We've no time to lose."

So they hurried out, and Gordon bumped into the hedgehog on its way into the police station.

"Ouch," said Gordon.

"Very important," said the hedgehog, "I must report a hare who was running so fast that I—"

Gordon raised his hand. "Not now," he said. "Important police investigation!"

"We have to find a mother!" squeaked Gertrude and Sune.

And off they went into the dark, making a beeline through the forest. The hedgehog could see how Buffy went first with a searchlight. Light played over the path. Then came the two young ones sharing an umbrella and holding smaller searchlights. And last of all, Gordon, carrying a very large backpack, and puffing.

Lucky they had the small police with them, Gordon thought, otherwise Buffy would be running so fast he could never keep up.

They went through the big forest and then the path led away up a mountain.

"That's the right way," puffed Gordon, still last.

Away from the forest cover, rain poured down on them and the wind took hold of the umbrella. The little ones were almost lifted up and blown away. Gordon clasped the umbrella to his heavy body and the young police walked beside him so as not to get so badly wet.

"It's hard work being police!" said Sune.

"And one is a little frightened of all the ghosts up here on the mountain," said Gertrude.

"Yes, one is a little scared," said Sune.

Gordon called out to Buffy that they must all sing a happy police song. It should be about how one must bravely keep moving forwards all the time. Carry on, carry on, and never give up, or something of the sort. Couldn't Buffy quickly write a song like that?

But Buffy could only think about her mother and how urgent their mission was, so this was the best she could do:

*Tramp, tramp, tramp and tramp.*
*Tramp, tramp and trampety-tramp.*

The song was easy to remember and easy to sing.
Buffy sang it first and the small police followed in their
squeaky voices. Gordon hummed like a big bumble
bee. It sounded very beautiful and comforting up there
on the mountain.

When all four had sung the song about fifteen times,
they felt a little braver and a little more energetic.
And then suddenly they weren't going uphill any more.

"We're on top of the mountain!" said Buffy. "Now
it's downhill all the way to the sea."

The wind grabbed hold of the umbrella and tumbled
it down the mountain.

"We'll get a bit wet," said Gordon. "But we'll be
even wetter quite soon."

So they sang the song one more time, only faster
now they were going down the hill.

*Tramp, tramp, tramp and tramp.*
*Tramp, tramp and trampety-tramp.*

*Tramp, tramp, tramp and tramp.*

*Tramp, tramp and trampety-tramp.*
*Tramp, tramp and trampety-tramp.*

And after that, another fifteen times. By then they were down the mountain, and in front of them was the sea. The sun came up after their long night of trudging. It stopped raining, but they were already soaked through. Away in the distance was an island. They could make out fir trees, a little mountain, and possibly a waterfall.

Cave Island.

# CHAPTER FIVE

## A snuggly blanket

They had a glimpse of Cave Island. But sea lay before it. The wind howled and the waves foamed.

"How shall we get across?" Gordon asked.

"We *must* get there," said Buffy.

"I can swim," said Sune. "As a toad I float very well."

"I am also a toad," said Gordon.

"I can take a little mouse on my head," said Sune.

"Me too," said Gordon.

So the two toads went into the water, Sune with a splash and Gordon very slowly and hesitantly. He was a real coward when it came to swimming. With great reluctance he got wet to his belly.

"Brrr. What did I say?" muttered Gordon. "We got wetter."

When he was in at last, the two mice stepped up onto the toads' heads. Buffy on Gordon and Gertrude on Sune.

The toads splashed away from the beach. They bounced in the wild sea and swam with determined strokes towards Cave Island.

By the time the mice finally stepped onto land they felt very seasick.

"That was—*burp*—horrible sailing on a toad—*ulk*—over the sea!" said Gertrude.

The toads also clambered ashore. They weren't seasick because they were used to water and waves.

They were all freezing, but Gertrude had a dry hand towel in her backpack and when they had dried themselves off and hopped around a little they warmed up.

There was a knobbly tree beside them on the beach with low-hanging branches. Buffy stared at it.

"I recognize that!" she burst out. "It was here! At first I thought of climbing it to escape from the fox…"

Gertrude took her hand. "Poor thing," she said. "But how could you forget all that?"

Buffy shrugged. "It was so terrible," she said. "It was a shock when it happened. All of it. Maybe we want to forget the things that are most terrible. And then I met Gordon and I had work and a bed. And a name. And everything was so good… But how could I forget my mother?"

Gertrude patted Buffy's hand. "We'll find her!"

They made their way together to the middle of the island. Carefully, because the fox could appear at any moment.

Buffy and Gertrude constantly sniffed the air. They had an excellent sense of smell compared to the two toads. But no, not even their noses could detect any traces of another animal.

"No fox," said Gertrude.

"No mice," said Buffy quietly. "It only smells of fir trees and ocean."

The island was completely quiet. No crows or gulls could be heard. No little birds either. If there were any animals they were hiding themselves well. There was no sound until they neared the middle of the island, when they heard the whoosh of a waterfall.

It had rained all night so there was plenty of water. It fell over a step and foamed and sizzled into eddies below.

"Was it here?" asked Gordon.

"What?"

"Was it here?" Gordon shouted louder over the noise.

Buffy nodded, then headed down a slope towards a big fir tree. The others followed as Buffy slipped beneath its tight and prickly branches. And then she stopped. She stood absolutely still within the hum of the tree.

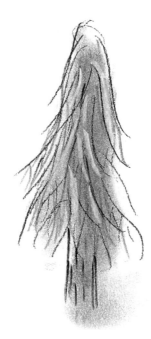

"It was here! Our little nest was here beneath the fir."
She began to tremble. Gertrude took her hand again.

Gordon went past them and looked down into an
open hole at the roots of the tree.

He stepped back and took a deep breath. "There's
only broken furniture left," he said.

He climbed awkwardly down into the hole. A broken
bed. An empty jar. A torn-apart cushion with down still
blowing around.

Hmm, he thought. No dead at least. No bones, skeletons or other terrible remains.

Buffy looked in.

"There!" she cried. "That's my bed! And there's…"

She scuttled down and scraped at one corner where there was a rag. Wet from the rain and dirty with earth. She pulled it into her arms and sniffed it. Great tears fell from her eyes.

"…my snuggly blanket. It has my smell! This is my old blanket."

# CHAPTER SIX

## No tracks, no clues—
## but a thought

Buffy held the blanket to her nose and closed her eyes as she rubbed it over her whiskers.

This had once been her home.

The roof was broken so you could see straight into the abandoned bedroom.

It used to be so beautiful. Oh, now Buffy remembered everything. Everything she'd forgotten in shock came back to her.

There was a small, well-hidden hole at the base of the fir tree. That was where you used to creep inside. Straight in, and a little to the left, was the toilet. A bit further on and to the right was the pantry, filled with nuts and nice small cones. In between was the big

living room where Mama and all the young ones lived.
All the beds were there in a row.

It was so lovely. Two children to each bed. They slept
top to tail, and before they settled down for the night
they lay awhile teasing each other and playing.
In the mornings they tugged at the covers,
trying to get as much of them as they could.
My cheeky sister, Buffy thought, and a tear ran
down her cheek. Sister or brother—you had
to wonder, since mouse children actually don't
have names.

In the morning they all sat on the edge of
the bed and Mama gave them each a nut. While
the children ate, she sang one of the songs well known
to mice. "Through Wild Snow, a Mouse on the Run"
or "In a Corner of Our Home Are Seven Kinds of
Cake."

Sometimes they went for a short walk after breakfast.
That was before the fox appeared on the island.

Once they met their father and they said hello nicely.
But he was very busy and about to go away. Yes, that's
how it was in the world of mice.

Then home they went. If Mama was still out
gathering nuts, the children would bounce on the

beds. High and higher. When Mama came home she was a little bit stern.

"I've told you before, you could hurt yourselves jumping on the beds. Let's dance instead!"

And so they sang the song "We Take Each Other by the Tail and Do the Circle Dance."

Sometimes Mama told them stories, like the one about the angry cat who was tricked by a tiny little mouse. The children hopped up and down in excitement. They longed for the end, when the cat fell in the water and the little mouse ran home with the cheese. They all laughed and clapped their hands.

What a wonderful childhood Buffy had had. And how much she loved her mother.

She started to cry when she realized everything the fox had destroyed.

Gordon also felt very moved.

"Imagine if the fox had got you! Then we would never have met. You would never have become such a clever police detective."

He cleared his throat and made a sort of speech.

"When a child dies, it is not just a cute, loveable little one who goes. In that instant, a potential police detective also disappears. It is not only the child who disappears, but also what that child might have become. It is doubly tragic and sad when a young one dies."

He was inspired and began again:

"In every child there is a whole world. The child must go on living. Otherwise there goes with it a world-famous singer, a sniffer, a talented stamper—and a dear friend and cake-eater also. And all the little one's children and grandchildren disappear as well. Thousands of mice that will never live! A tragedy!"

Sune gave Gordon a slight poke in the bottom. "But she isn't dead," he said.

Gordon cleared his throat again.

"No," he said at last. "I was feeling angry about the terrible damage a fox can do. If we'd had our stamp here we would have certainly done some stamping!"

Then he remembered that he himself, Gordon, had caused everything. He was the one who'd driven the fox out of his own police district. Hmm, very important: If you simply drive your danger away, it becomes someone else's danger.

Gordon went over to Buffy and hugged her and said in a choking voice: "I am so sorry your mother is gone. What sorrow…"

"Wait a minute," said Sune.

"Can't we stop and think a little," said Gertrude. "You said that's what police should do."

They sat in a circle. Gordon was still feeling moved. Buffy sniffed her blanket.

"How many beds were here?" asked Gertrude.

"Eight," said Buffy. "Two young ones in each. Yes, and Mama of course…"

"There's only one bed still here," said Sune. "Yours. The one that was broken when the fox struck. Could someone else have come and taken the others later? Who though?"

They all thought.

"Mama and the other youngsters!" Gordon said with a smile.

"Or other mice," said Buffy, distressed.

Gertrude shook her head. "How many snuggly blankets did you have?"

"All the children had their own…"

"And how many are still here?"

Buffy turned over her blanket and looked at it. "Only mine," she said. "Do you mean that my brothers and sisters took their own? And only mine was left? And they think I'm the one who was eaten up?"

Sune nodded.

Gordon had cheered up. "Well," he said, "that all sounds good, but these are only thoughts. We can be a little hopeful, but we must investigate further. What shall we do?"

Buffy folded up her blanket and put it away.

"First we must sniff out the entire area," she said, "to be certain there are no mice here. Then I'll explain what we should do next."

They all climbed up out of the hole and Buffy and Gertrude began to sniff their way around. There was not much mouse smell. But it had rained such a lot in the night, so it didn't necessarily mean no mice.

"No tracks, no clues," said Gordon. "But a good thought from the small police, which gives us hope. What shall we do now, Buffy?"

"Put on your nice new police hats," said Buffy.

Gertrude and Sune's paper hats had become a little soggy in the rain. But Gertrude had more in her backpack.

Buffy inspected the three police in front of her.

"I don't think he'll attack police," she said. "That's why it's important to wear our hats. Now we'll sniff him out. And interrogate him."

"Who?" said Gertrude.

"The fox," said Buffy.

# Interrogation protocol: the fox

Four police went off to investigate, their gold-starred hats shining in the sun. They marched in time around the whole island. The two talented sniffers went first.

When they had covered the entire island except for the furthest headland, the sniffers found a track.

"Fox," said Buffy. "Fox ahead!"

Gordon suggested that he be the one to question the fox. Buffy was too distressed. In an interrogation one must be polite and correct, not angry and upset.

Buffy understood.

They went on through the sparse forest and the pungent smell of fox grew stronger. Gertrude even had to hold her nose.

At last they reached a big rock and there on the other side was a fox, very fast asleep.

They crept closer to him. Buffy whispered that they should stand at attention beside the fox.

Gordon then took a step forward. "Hrmm." He cleared his throat. "What have we here then?"

The fox opened one eye and looked at Gordon. Then he closed it again.

# Interrogation protocol: the fox

## 8.15 a.m.

*(Recorded at the police station later)*

GORDON: Hmm. Unfortunately we must interrogate you about an event last winter.

*Gordon was speaking very properly. The fox sat up. Its coat was red and glinted in the sunshine.*

FOX: What do you mean, what sort of event?

GORDON: It concerns the case of an assault on a mouse family who lived over at the waterfall. This is prohibited!

FOX: Ha! How could it be prohibited?

BUFFY: Pfft.

*Buffy started jumping up and down with rage. She breathed deeply so she wouldn't shriek out loud.*

GORDON: It is the law. *Act of Special Importance.* Clause 2. The second most important paragraph. We must also determine whether any animals have been eaten up. Absolutely forbidden! Clause 1. The most important paragraph of all.

*The fox looked down at the ground. Then he looked closely at Gordon.*

FOX: I recognize you. Wasn't it you who forced me to leave the forest?

GORDON: Yes, anyone who eats others cannot stay in my police district.

FOX: You told me I'd have to eat you if I disobeyed.

GORDON: Yes.

*Gordon puffed himself up until he was completely round.*

FOX: Well, I don't eat disgusting toads. Only birds and mice. Ideally small mice.

GERTRUDE: Hmpff! You wouldn't dare eat me. I'm the POLICE!

FOX: I never eat anything I've spoken to. One doesn't want to converse with one's food.

GERTRUDE: So if you're going to eat someone up, they should start talking to you?

FOX: In that case I'd close my ears. I am cunning.

*Gordon interrupted, anxious to get to the important question.*

GORDON: Did you or did you not ambush a mouse nest beside the waterfall?

FOX: Maybe…well, sure I did. I have to eat.

GERTRUDE: Can't you eat *dead* animals? Old snakes, already dead.

*The fox would not answer the question.*

GERTRUDE: Can't you eat nuts?

FOX: Don't be an idiot! Nuts!

GERTRUDE: No swearing!

FOX: That's not food for a fox. Nuts and grass. That's not natural!

GERTRUDE: Buy butter, then.

FOX: No money.

GERTRUDE: Fish?

FOX: Don't like water.

GERTRUDE: Are you afraid of water?

FOX: A little, perhaps. One's coat gets so wet and heavy.

*Silence. Gertrude looked very carefully at the fox.*

GERTRUDE: You have a very beautiful coat. That lovely white on your chest. May I feel it?

*The fox nodded.*

GERTRUDE: You won't eat the police, will you?

FOX: You don't trust me, huh?

*He giggled.*

GERTRUDE: Na—ya.

*Gertrude went up close and patted the fox's chest.*

GERTRUDE: Very soft and white and beautiful. I'd like a coat like yours.

FOX: Thank you.

GERTRUDE: I might like being a big, strong fox like you. But no, actually, I feel sorry for you. You can't be in the club.

FOX: What club? What club can't I be in?

GERTRUDE: Everyone living in the forest is a member. If they believe in the law.

GORDON: She means citizens, not members!

GERTRUDE: But maybe you belong to a different club. For those who eat animals. Eagles, wolves and so on.

FOX: No, we don't have a club. We…ah, we'd just end up eating each other.

GORDON: This whole thing is very sad. But I don't see that there's any solution.

BUFFY: Pfft.

*Buffy was jumping up and down. She had her hand over*
*her mouth, but she couldn't wait any longer. She had to ask*
*the question even if Gordon thought she was rude.*

BUFFY: HAVE YOU EATEN MY MOTHER?

*She screamed it with such fury that they all jumped.*
*The fox looked at her and took a step closer to sniff her.*

FOX: Were you the one who ran away, straight onto the
  ice? You were really fast.

*Buffy nodded.*

FOX: Rats! Everyone blames me for everything!
  I'm not talking to you…

*Buffy began to cry. The fox seemed embarrassed and ashamed.*

BUFFY: I'll be really sad if you've eaten my mother.

*Silence.*

FOX: No, I swear, I had nothing to eat that day. I was so hungry my stomach ached and grumbled.

No, the mice are probably still there somewhere. I smell them sometimes, but I have no idea where they are…

Now the interrogation was complete, Buffy didn't know what to do.

"Thank you," she said.

She made a salute, turned around and marched off.

The two small police also saluted and followed her.

Gordon said, "I hope we police never have to interrogate you again. Sa-lute! March!"

"What should I eat?" said the fox.

Gordon had no answer. He just kept going.

# CHAPTER EIGHT

# Where is the cave at Cave Island?

Gordon ran to catch up with the others. They were on their way to the waterfall to sniff again, really, really carefully.

"Your mother is alive," Gordon puffed.

"If we can trust the fox," said Buffy harshly.

"I trust him," said Gertrude. "And I feel sorry for him."

Gordon settled on a rock beside the falls. Sune sat next to him. After all, they couldn't do much else while the mice were sniffing around for evidence.

"Shall we have a little cake?" Gordon began to open the backpack. "I have almond dreams, sugar tops and strawberry whirls. Which do you want?"

Sune couldn't choose. He knew he didn't want a sugar top, because you had to wash your face and hands afterwards. Hmm. Maybe strawberry…

He was about to say so when Gordon zipped the backpack up again.

"No, probably we should save the cake till we've found Buffy's mother," he said.

Sune looked at him, wondering what he meant.

"It is always good to have a little reward," Gordon explained. "First we find her mother and then we have cake! It makes us think faster and more wisely."

"Are we *thinking* out where she is?" Sune asked.

Gordon nodded. He felt they knew enough now to figure out where she was. Just by thinking.

"Hmm." Sune leaned his head in his hands like a real thinker. He sat perfectly still for a moment.

"It's hard to think," he said. "Can't you help me?"

"Well, here are a few questions. Are her mother and siblings alive?"

"Yes," said Sune.

"Are they far away?"

"No," said Sune. "There's sometimes a whiff of them here. The fox said so."

"Where are they, then?"

Sune stood up and looked in all directions but saw nothing.

Then Buffy and Gertrude came back. They sat down, disappointed. There were no clues to be found.

Sune had an idea.

"Maybe I could write a poem, the way police officers do."

"Why not," said Gordon. "You might as well. Maybe you can catch a thought that is inside you."

Sune thought for a long time. Everyone looked at him. At last he said:

*Where is the cave*
*where we can find our knave (our rat)?*

"Knave! Rat!" Buffy exclaimed. "My mother's not a knave-rat, she's the cutest mouse there is."

Sune blushed. "I couldn't find another rhyme…"

"Aha," said Gordon, "but you don't have to rhyme in these poems. Try to catch your thought again. There'll be cake!"

Sune said:

*Where is the cave*
*at Cave Island?*

The island was called Cave Island, so there must be a cave on it, otherwise it would be strange. They had gone around the whole island, though, and hadn't seen the slightest trace of a cave.

"Bravo," they all told Sune, who blushed again.

"We are getting close to something important," said Gordon. "We should not look for a mother. We should look for a cave that is protected from foxes. Where is she? Where is the cave, Sune?"

Sune sat like a thinker again, with his head on his hand. And then he used both hands. He began breathing fast as if he were angry or about to lift a heavy weight. He squeezed his eyes shut.

"Thinking is hard work," said Gordon.

Sune stood up. He said in a clear voice:

*The fox is afraid of just one thing.*
*His coat gets wet in water.*

Sune breathed out and sat down. The others thought carefully about the poem.

"Yes!" they all exclaimed. "You've thought it out, Sune!"

"Can I have cake now?" he asked. "The strawberry whirl?"

"As soon as we've found her..."

Where exactly would the cave be, they all wondered.

Gertrude got up. She took Buffy's hand and pulled her along; they went straight towards the creek, straight to the waterfall.

Beside the creek was a narrow outcrop of rock where you could walk without getting your feet wet. The two mouse police went right into the waterfall. The curtain of water poured down over them.

And then they disappeared.

# CHAPTER NINE

# Much hugging and licking

The curtain of water fell over Buffy and Gertrude. It almost pushed them to the ground. But they went right through it and found themselves in a large, dark cave.

"Hello!" Buffy cried, and the echo answered, "Ello, ello, ello!"

When her eyes had adjusted, she saw that the cave was full of beds, pillows and blankets.

A little mouse came up to her.

"But it's you!" Buffy cried.

Yes, it was the sister she'd shared a bed with.

"I knew you were alive," said her sister. "I was waiting for you."

"My little sister," said Buffy, crying and hugging her.

Gertrude saw that they were exactly alike, with the same expressions on their faces, the same voices and the same clothes.

"My mother! All my brothers and sisters!"

Yes, there was her mother in the dark cave. And there were her fifteen children. Half of them were big brothers and sisters to Buffy, but the younger ones had caught up, so now they were all the same size.

Buffy was still wearing her police hat. She rushed up to her mother and sniffed her.

"Oh, my mother's own beautiful smell," she said with a sigh.

"You're alive!" said her mother joyfully. "Where have you been?"

"And what about you? Have you been here in the cave all along?" asked Buffy.

They hugged. Then they licked each other. Buffy was wet in the face and happy.

Now Gordon and Sune also entered the cave. They each held their breath as they ran through the waterfall.

"Terrible," said Gordon, snorting. "You small police are very clever!"

"The cave was very close by indeed," said Sune. "Just as I thought."

They could see Buffy and her mother licking each other's faces. Buffy's police hat had fallen to the ground.

"Hmm, mice will be mice," Gordon whispered to Sune. "We toads would never lick each other."

Buffy rushed on and squeezed and licked all her siblings.

Gordon was very touched, but nevertheless tried to behave like a chief detective. He walked up to Buffy's mother and took her solemnly by the hand.

"Pleased to meet you. My name is Chief Detective Gordon. I am a police colleague of Buffy's."

"Buffy? Who?" said her mother.

Of course, this mother didn't know that Gordon had given her child the name of Buffy.

"Buffy, your lost child," said Gordon. "She is certainly not a child any longer. She is the Chief of Police in the woods. A very important police detective."

The mother began to cry with joy. "I'm so happy and proud. But how did you find us?"

"Normal police work," said Gordon.

"We thought and then we wrote police poems," said Sune standing next to him.

He had picked up Buffy's hat and put it on his own head on top of his little police hat. So that no one would stand on it, he said.

It took some time for the four police to greet Buffy's mother and all of Buffy's brothers and sisters. But after

sixty-eight handshakes, hugs or lickings, this was done, and they could all sit down on the beds holding each other's hands and talking over the top of each other.

"Buffy," said Gordon, "perhaps we could serve some little cakes. Buffy!"

No one was listening to him and he suddenly realized that here in the cave were a sea of Buffys! All the mice children looked exactly the same with matching clothes.

He tapped one of them on the shoulder. "Buffy?"

The little mouse nodded in surprise.

"Are you Buffy?

"Who's Buffy?" said the mouse in exactly the same voice as Buffy's.

Well, who was Buffy? He went on to the next.

"Buffy?"

"Yes!" said the little mouse. "Yes, I'd also like to be called Buffy."

"Me too!" said the mouse sitting beside her.

"And me?" said a third. "Buffy is a beautiful name."

"Hmm," said Gordon. "It is probably not a good idea to all have the same name..."

How would he find his best friend among all these twins, a cave full of twins!

"Shouldn't we eat cakes?" said Sune. "We can of
course salute all the mice and then offer them cakes."

Yes! If Gordon called out that all police officers
should salute, they would discover the correct Buffy.

"All police, salute!" called Gordon, and the cave
echoed, "alute, alute, alute!"

Four police officers stood up. And there was Buffy!

"Quick, put the hat on her," Gordon whispered to
Sune.

Then he gave a little speech.

"Dear mice, at our police station in the forest,
we usually eat very delicious cakes. With us now we
have almond dreams with a sprinkle of chocolate.
We have strawberry whirls—with cream inside and
half a strawberry on top. We also have sugar tops, made

with wonderful deep-fried dough dipped in powdered sugar."

"Warning, warning!" said Sune. "You have to wash yourself afterwards!"

"By the way, I have a lot of lovely hats for everyone in my backpack," said Gertrude.

She shared out blue paper hats. They had writing on their gold stars. What did it say? *Police* perhaps.

When this was done, Gordon cleared his throat.

"Finally, everyone gets to choose the cake they would like!"

He opened the backpack and looked inside. There at the bottom was a shapeless blob. A cake blob. Water had got into the pack and everything had mixed together into a dough.

He sighed, but suddenly had a solution.

"I have a better idea," he said. "Everyone gets a lump of cake, with a little mix of everything."

He dug into his backpack and shaped lumps, as big as snowballs, one each for everyone.

"Strawberry almond with chocolate sugar cream," he said.

Everyone was very pleased and satisfied.

# To escape from the fox

Yes, it was a real party! Buffy and her mother sat stroking each other, smiling.

"I think we need to go home now," said Gordon, "otherwise the parents of the small police will be worried. It was nice that we found you and very good to know that everything is fine."

Buffy's mother looked at him. "But everything is not fine!" she said. "Fox is horrible! We thought you had come to save us."

"Oops," said Gordon. "I didn't understand."

"Chief Detective Gordon," said Buffy, standing up. "I think we should take them home with us to the forest."

"Chief Detective Buffy," said Gordon. "So we should! That is exactly what we responsible toads and mice must do. But where should they live? It's getting cold, and there's not room in the prison." Gordon stopped at once when he saw the mother's horrified expression. "Yes, our snug little former prison..."

Now Gertrude began to jump up and down. She saluted and said, "We small police have found many uninhabited holes where they can live."

Gordon saluted her back. "Good, then we can set off immediately! But how will we cross the water?

Sune now spoke up to say, "I noticed a small boat tied to a stake. Just off the beach. We can swim to it."

One of Buffy's siblings explained that the boat was theirs. The oars were hidden in a shrub on dry land. But they had not used the boat for a long time, because they were a little scared.

"Bravo! Let's go!"

But the mother still had objections. "We don't dare," she said. "Fox is here, outside. He'll eat us up."

Gordon pondered.

"We have police hats for each of us, so I don't think the fox will eat us," suggested Gertrude.

*Think*, thought Gordon. Sometimes you want to not only think, but also know. Especially when it comes to being eaten up. But he said nothing. He might think of something if the fox appeared. Or should he be more worried?

He stood between Gertrude and Sune, took off their police hats and put his hands on their heads. One hand on Sune's bare and smooth, slightly chilly

head. The other hand on Gertrude's soft warm fur.

"My fine small police!" he said, and he put their hats back on.

And off they went. Buffy went first, looking and sniffing. No, there was no hint of fox on the air. A long line of mice came after her. Each was carrying a pillow. They all walked down to the beach where the boat was moored.

They stood with the wind in their faces. Buffy sniffed. No, still no smell of fox.

Suddenly Gertrude caught a glimpse of something behind them. What was moving in the bushes? No, no smell. Who was approaching *against* the wind so they wouldn't notice?

"Fox!" cried Gertrude, pointing.

Yes, there he was! The fox was sneaking quietly over, wriggling like an eel on bent legs, his bushy tail hidden in the grass.

"Hello there!" cried Gertrude. "We're just the police. Twenty police officers with lovely hats."

But the fox did not hear. He approached rapidly and opened his mouth.

"It's just us, and we're talking to you! We're not food," she cried again.

But the fox didn't care.

"Help, he's closed his ears!"

They had to save themselves. Otherwise all the poor mice would be eaten up this fine morning on Cave Island.

"Let's run back!" cried one lot of mice.

"No, there's no time. He'll catch us," cried another lot.

Things were looking very bad.

Gordon and Sune looked at each other and nodded.

There was one thing the fox was afraid of.

"Into the water!" they shouted.

"No, he'll catch us there!" answered the mice.

"Don't worry! He's scared of water."

And just as the fox was about to snatch the nearest mouse, they jumped straight into the water. Plop.

The fox turned around and tried to snap up some of the others. But they also threw themselves into the waves. Plop. Plop. They tried to keep the pillows above their heads. Ah well, if the pillows got wet they could dry them again. It was a matter of life and death.

The fox ran for Buffy's mother and some others. But they jumped in, right in front of his snout. Plop. Plop plop.

"Rats," snapped the fox.

Now all the mice were in the water.

Sune jumped in too; he swam for the boat. It was not so far away.

Gordon was left alone on the beach. The fox ran to the water's edge and stopped short, so as not to wet his feet. He howled his disappointment.

"Listen here, Fox," said Gordon. "We're leaving now. I'll just get the oars."

But the fox was cross and gnashed at the air with his sharp teeth.

"Better watch out," said Gordon, "or I'll jump right into your mouth. I'll be the most disgusting thing you ever ate!"

The fox snapped his mouth shut.

"Look out. Here I come, ready to be eaten! Mo-ho-ho-ho," said Gordon spookily.

The fox backed away, terrified.

Gordon didn't know quite what to feel. Glad he'd outwitted the fox? Or hurt that not even a hungry fox wanted to eat a disgusting toad like himself?

In the meantime, the mice had launched the boat.

Gordon carried the oars to the water. He carefully put one toe in. Oh, it was cold.

He stopped. Too scared to get in? He walked slowly, shivering, into the water. He swam out and was pulled up into the boat by many small, strong mouse arms.

The boat was so full of mice that his big body was pushed and squashed down between Gertrude and the stern.

"You should never trust the fox," Gordon told her.

"Well, I do trust him," she replied. "He never actually said that he wouldn't eat the police. He didn't *lie*."

Gertrude pulled cheese sandwiches out of her backpack. She threw them onto the beach.

A small boat, full of eighteen mice and two toads, made its way slowly over the sea.

They had left Cave Island.

The fox sniffed the sandwiches.

"I'll send you my fishing rod once I'm home," Gertrude cried, and she waved.

## Hop, hop, hop and hop

The autumn sun was shining when the boat landed
on the beach at the other side. Two toads and eighteen
mice stepped onto land, forming a long line and
carrying their wet pillows. They all climbed the hill on
their way home to the forest.

Buffy wrote a new song. The same tune as before,
but much happier.

*Hop, hop, hop and hop.*
*Hop, hop, hoppity hop.*

Going home was much faster. It was such a joy that everyone had been found and rescued from the fox. They no longer had to sit trapped in a damp cave. Now they would each get a nice dry burrow, the ones found by the small police.

They went up the hill, full speed down the mountain, and into the forest. Gordon came last, puffing and leaning on Sune.

After an hour or so, they were back in their own piece of forest. And soon they could see the police station.

But what was this? Many animals were gathered outside the police station. The hedgehog was there, and around him were a lot of squirrels and rabbits, mice and crows.

They cheered when the long line of animals approached.

"Have you rescued the mother?" cried the hedgehog.

"Yes," answered Gordon. "And all her children!"

What a loud hurrah there was!

"Bravo," they cried. "Long live the police!"

"And the small police too," said Buffy.

"Long live the small police!" cried all the animals.

And they began to sing and throw hats in the air. What a fantastic party! All that was missing was an orchestra.

"Welcome, you there," said the hedgehog to a mouse. "And you!"

Gordon clapped his hands and said he had something important to say.

"All the mice must have names," he said. "It is important to be someone. You can't just be 'you there' or 'you.' So we must think of some lovely names."

"Sunshine," called someone.

"Blueberry and Birchleaves, Raspberry and Morning Breeze."

So many fine suggestions!

All the mice were now choosing their names. Two wanted Blueberry and the one who didn't get it was a little cross, even though she was given Rowanberry instead. And it suited her well.

But what would the mother be called?

"Summer," cried Buffy.

A better name it was not possible to find. After all, it could be said that summer is the mother of sunshine, blueberries and the morning breeze.

Then it was time for everyone to find their holes. The small police ran ahead pointing them out and handing out searchlights. Summer should live close to the police station, they decided.

All the animals who'd met up at the station rushed off to collect things to give to the mice: a stool, a frying pan, a piece of apple cake, an ornamental pig and a wall hanging with *Home Sweet Home* embroidered on it in crooked letters.

Gordon was so tired that he sat down under a tree to rest. Buffy sat next to him.

"Thank you, dear Gordon," she said. "Thank you for coming with me, thank you for going on and on even though you must have been really tired."

Gordon couldn't hold back a yawn. "You have to go on and on," he said. "Never give up! We are the police."

He closed his eyes. "But now I want to sleep."

"I've been given the best thing of all," said Buffy.
"The thing that every small mouse longs for: to be
Chief Inspector. And to have my mother close by."

But Gordon had fallen asleep and was snoring loudly.

"Oh well," said Buffy. "You may sleep a little,
but then we have to go in and do some stamping with
the small police. And we have some important things to
decide..."

# CHAPTER TWELVE

# The very last chapter— coconut puffs

It was afternoon in the woods and the four friends sat at the desk, drinking a cup of tea.

"Is the Police Academy finished now?" asked Gertrude.

"The small police school is over," said Gordon. "You've done very well and been a lot of help."

Gertrude went over to the great Book of Law lying on a table. She felt it and tried to pick it up, but only managed to raise it by one corner.

"I thought we were going to learn the whole Book of Law."

"Can you read then?" asked Gordon, his head to one side.

"No, maybe not really," said Gertrude. "And I was wondering how to get that very big book into my small head. It won't fit."

"When you grow up you should become real police officers," said Buffy. "Then we'll go through the law book."

Sune stood up and said, "Except that *everyone* is the police. I said that to the hedgehog. And he understood. All members want to help."

"Citizens," Gordon corrected him.

Buffy went to get a box of cakes she'd been keeping in the bookshelf.

"Please have a taste," she said. "Here we have banana cake with crispy sugar topping, and nougat rolls with mint chips. And these are the tiny coconut puffs."

Everyone tasted all the different kinds of cake and then ate the cakes they thought were the best. Pretty soon the coconut puffs were gone.

"Thank you," said Buffy. "Now we've voted for which cakes we should buy!"

"Voted?" said Gordon.

"Yes, we've eaten up the cakes we like the best. I'm going to order a lot of coconut puffs, quite a few nougat rolls and a couple of banana cakes."

Gordon nodded. It was a very good decision, he thought.

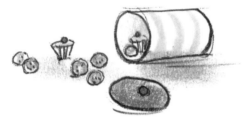

Buffy wrote it down on a piece of paper, took out the stamp and placed it on the paper. She moved it a little to the right, then a little to the left. Everyone put their hands on the stamp and pushed. KLA-DUNK.

"Now we must just write down a few pieces of wisdom," said Gordon. "That's what police do."

He took a piece of paper and at the top, he wrote: *A Case for Buffy*.

"Or a case for the small police," Sune said.

"But it's about Buffy's mother and that is the most important thing."

Gertrude and Sune agreed.

"Go on and write a few wise words, small police officers!" said Gordon.

They each wrote to their heart's content. Long complicated sentences with fat round dots at the end.

"What does it say?" said Sune, handing the paper to Gordon.

"Hmm," said Gordon, turning the paper this way and that. "I think it says that you must think about a poem and write it down."

"That's right," said Sune. "A police poem."

"What does it say on mine?" Gertrude gave her paper to Buffy.

"Hmm," said Buffy. "In every child there is a whole world. That's what it says."

And so all together they stamped the wise words. KLA-DUNK. KLA-DUNK. Gordon put all three pieces of paper in the drawer for important notes. The paper about cakes was also quite wise, he thought.

"Now you need to go home to your mothers!" said Buffy.

"Thank you very much," said Gordon.

But Gertrude wouldn't go.

"Wait," she said. "We never found out what a small mouse would do with an old badger who said 'Snot child.' Would the mouse be cross?"

"Or would he cry, like I said?" Sune asked.

"Hmm," said Gordon. "I don't know. But think of Buffy and the fox. What made the fox talk?"

"Buffy cried," said Sune happily.

"Sometimes it's best. Although the police can't always go around crying."

Now the two small police put on their backpacks.

"Don't forget to send your fishing rod to the fox," said Gordon to Gertrude. "I thought that you small police might find a solution. We cannot always be enemies with the fox."

Gertrude and Sune stopped in the doorway and made a salute. "Let's play again tomorrow."

Now Detective Gordon and Detective Buffy were on their own.

Gordon got into his comfortable flannel pajamas.

"I must go to bed," he said. "I shall think about our small wisdoms. And perhaps have a small sleep. I am very pleased that we had the small police academy. That means there will be police who can take over when we can't manage any longer… There will always be new police. And I have the feeling that they will be even better. Good night."

But Buffy stayed up, whistling a little to herself.
It was only the afternoon. Time for more afternoon tea,
perhaps?

She put all the remaining cakes into a box.

And then she sneaked out like a real chief detective
while Gordon was snoring loudly.

Buffy could go and visit her mother with cakes.

She whistled happily all the way.

The sweet little
police station

Vacant hole for
someone to live in

A boat for twenty small animals to travel home in

The fox. Aiee!

Cave Island (But where is the cave?)

The tree Buffy remembers

The high mountain

But it was much higher than that, I think, says Sune)

This is where you swim over

Map of Detective Gordon and Detective Buffy's police district

(and Gertrude and Sune's)

DETECTIVE GORDON · DETECTIVE BUFFY

This edition first published in 2018 by Gecko Press
PO Box 9335, Wellington 6141, New Zealand
info@geckopress.com

English-language edition © Gecko Press Ltd 2018
Original title: *Kommissarie Gordon: Ett fall för Paddy*
Text © Ulf Nilsson 2017
Illustrations © Gitte Spee 2017
First published by Bonnier Carlsen Bokförlag, Stockholm, Sweden
Published in the English language by arrangement with
Bonnier Rights, Stockholm, Sweden

Distributed in the United States and Canada by
Lerner Publishing Group, lernerbooks.com
Distributed in the United Kingdom by
Bounce Sales and Marketing, bouncemarketing.co.uk
Distributed in Australia by Scholastic Australia, scholastic.com.au
Distributed in New Zealand by Upstart Distribution, upstartpress.co.nz

Translated by Julia Marshall
Edited by Penelope Todd
Cover design by Vida & Luke Kelly, New Zealand
Typesetting by Katrina Duncan
Printed in China by Everbest Printing Co. Ltd,
an accredited ISO 14001 & FSC certified printer

ISBN hardback: 978-1-776571-78-9 (USA)
ISBN paperback: 978-1-776571-79-6
Ebook available

For more curiously good books, visit geckopress.com